Face Lift

Paul Blum

RISING STARS

NASEN House, 4/5 Amber Business Village, Amber Close,
Amington, Tamworth, Staffordshire, B77 4RP

Rising Stars UK Ltd.
7 Hatchers Mews, Bermondsey Street, London SE1 3GS
www.risingstars-uk.com

Published 2012

Cover design: Burville-Riley Partnership
Brighton photographs: iStock
Illustrations: Chris King for Illustration Ltd (characters and cover artwork)/
Abigail Daker (map) http://illustratedmaps.info
Text design and typesetting: Geoff Rayner
Publisher: Rebecca Law
Editorial manager: Sasha Morton Creative Project Management

British Library Cataloguing in Publication Data.
A CIP record for this book is available from the British Library.

ISBN: 978-0-85769-601-4

Printed and bound by CPI Group (UK) Ltd, Croydon, CR0 4YY

Contents

Name:
John Logan

Age:
24

Hometown:
Manchester

Occupation:
Author of supernatural thrillers

Special skills:
Not yet known

Name:
Rose Petal

Age:
22

Hometown:
Brighton

Occupation:
Yoga teacher, nightclub and shop owner, vampire hunter

Special skills:
Private investigator specialising in supernatural crime

Location map
DUKE STREET
MIDDLE STREET
NORTH STREET
SHIP STREET
1
MIDDLE STREET
PRINCE ALBERT ST.
SHIP STREET
BARTHOLOMEWS AV.
BARTHOLOMEWS
EAST STREET
2
KINGS ROAD
Brighton, East Sussex

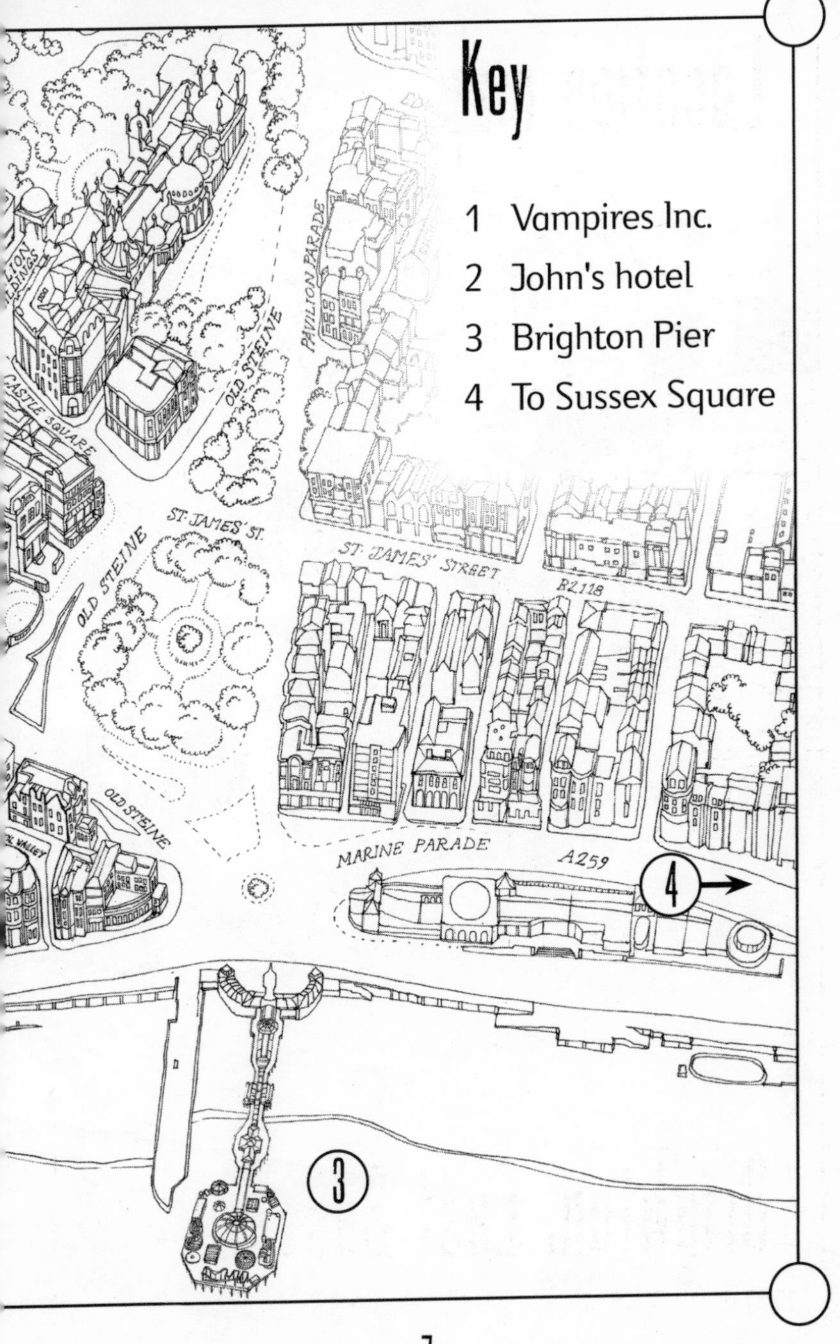

Key
1 Vampires Inc.
2 John's hotel
3 Brighton Pier
4 To Sussex Square
PAVILION PARADE
CASTLE SQUARE
OLD STEINE
ST. JAMES' ST.
OLD STEINE
ST. JAMES' STREET
OLD STEINE
MARINE PARADE
A259
4
3

Chapter 1

Linda left work at seven o'clock. It was a stormy night. She could smell the sea and hear the gulls screeching in the dark. Linda took a short cut to her home from the surgery. She went through the private garden in the middle of Sussex Square that only keyholders could enter.

Work had been quiet, but Dr Jacobs, her brother, was still in a good mood. He had worked for nearly ten years as a plastic surgeon in Brighton. People booked appointments to see him months in advance. They paid him thousands of pounds to look young and beautiful again. Linda always saw satisfied customers. No wonder her brother was so happy.

Suddenly, Linda heard footsteps behind her. She locked the gate quickly. The garden railings were too high for anyone to climb over – nobody could follow her now. She walked fast, but then she saw a cloaked figure coming towards her. There was no time to run away. Linda saw its face coming out of the shadows. It was a face she would never forget: the face of a monster!

The creature from the shadows held her tightly. 'Hello, Linda. You must remember me,' she whispered. The monster bit deep into Linda's neck and drank her blood slowly.

Linda could not fight the creature off. Her heartbeat slowed, slowed, stopped. The killer laid her on the grass and spoke softly as she stroked Linda's hair. 'Now your brother must learn to live with sadness and despair. Just like the sadness and despair he gave to me.'

The killer stepped away from the woman's body. For once, her face was flushed with colour. The thrill of the kill made life worth living. And this was just the first of three special kills she had planned.

****

It was seven in the morning and Rose Petal – yoga teacher and private investigator – was meditating. She felt totally peaceful until her mobile phone started to ring. Within moments, Rose was running down the stairs of Vampires Inc., the base for her supernatural detective agency, to a new crime scene.

On her way, Rose rang John Logan. John was a writer and Rose was helping him to research his new book. John wrote about the supernatural and Rose lived among the creatures he had thought were just fiction. He was starting to learn that they were actually real. John wouldn't want to miss another murder case.

By 7.30am, Rose and John were studying the body of Linda Jacobs. Rose took photos and examined the victim for clues. The police called Rose in when there were signs of a supernatural killing. Based on the bite marks on Linda's neck, this murder was the work of a vampire.

'Look, John. I've found strands of hair in Linda's watch. The police lab will be pleased to have something to work with,' she said. Rose handed her police contact an evidence bag. He nodded his thanks and jumped into his car with the siren blaring. Rose would get the results within twenty-four hours. There was no time to lose.

Chapter 2

A storm was building out at sea. The wind was lashing at the windows of the big, old house. The monster looked at herself in one of the many mirrors on the wall. A vampire can see its own reflection, even if human beings cannot. Even after ten years, she still shuddered every time she caught sight of herself.

'The doctor promised that I would be young again,' she said out loud. She pulled at the grey hair on her head. It came away in her hand. 'The doctor promised me that I would be beautiful again.' She scratched at the skin on her cheeks. It flaked away like dust.

'I am immortal. I must live like this forever,' she screamed. She picked up a hammer and smashed all the mirrors in the room. 'Now I will do to you what he has done to me!'

In a corner of the candlelit room, a teenage girl was tied to a chair. A gag stopped her from shouting for help. She closed her eyes as the monster raged, and wept.

****

Dr Jacobs was in a state of shock when Rose and John arrived at his house the next day. His sister had been killed and overnight his daughter, Helen, had gone missing.

'Thank you for seeing us at such a difficult time, Dr Jacobs,' Rose said. 'The police are doing everything they can, but I have skills that are useful in cases like this. Could you tell us about your family?'

'Linda worked as my receptionist. She came to the surgery about ten years ago,' explained the doctor as he paced up and down the room. 'In fact, Helen's mother used to work with us too. Sadly, she died nearly five years ago.'

'May I ask how your first wife died, Dr Jacobs?' said Rose.

'She killed herself,' said Jacobs in a very low voice. 'We never found out why. The police think she jumped off

Brighton Pier. They found her body at high tide.'

'Dr Jacobs,' said Rose, 'do you know why your wife took her own life?'

Max Jacobs shook his head. 'I have asked myself that question every day since she died,' he said. John caught Rose's eye. She looked bothered by something.

'Has anybody ever complained about their new face?' asked Logan.

'No, I don't think so,' said Dr Jacobs. Rose watched him closely as he spoke. She could tell that Dr Jacobs was lying. But why?

****

BRIGHTON
GIFTS

Back at Vampires Inc., John updated his website while Rose waited at the back door for a visitor. The results of the hair sample found on Linda Jacobs's watch were in. Rose had called a friend to help with the case. It was Alex Reddy, a rock star who was also her former boyfriend and a vampire.

Logan felt down. He didn't like Alex Reddy. He was way too cool and handsome for a dead bloke. John's worst fear was that Alex might persuade Rose to become a vampire. John told himself he was being stupid, but he couldn't help worrying about her. He was glad when she and Alex walked into the bar and sat down next to him.

'Alright, John?' smiled Alex. He knew John didn't like him. Rose nudged John to shake Alex's hand. John did so, then wiped his hand on his jeans.

'I've called Alex in because it seems that the hair sample from Linda Jacobs's watch belongs to a member of his own vampire family,' said Rose.

'There is a particular code that we Elder vampires have in our hair, nails and blood. It means we can identify a real Elder if one tries to join our "family",' said Alex. 'Being an Elder means we are immortal. We rarely feed and don't live close to other vampires. It is odd to find an Elder in Brighton. There are too many other supernatural creatures living here. It is even odder for an Elder to hunt and kill like this.'

'We all agree that Max Jacobs's daughter going missing is no coincidence,' said Rose. 'It seems that this Elder vampire has a grudge against the Jacobs family. He is picking them off, one by one. First Linda, now Helen. Maybe even Helen's mother, five years ago.'

'Shouldn't we be watching Max Jacobs, then?' asked John. He looked at Alex and Rose, who were sitting very close together. They made a good-looking couple. Knowing that Alex was going to live forever made John feel even more fed up.

'Alex has sent two of his band members to watch Dr Jacobs's surgery and house. We'll do the next shift in the morning. For now, I'm going to hack into Dr Jacobs's computer records and see what I can find out about his patients,' replied Rose. 'Alex will help me. You might as well get a good night's sleep, John. Meet me back here in the morning. Our stake-out shift starts at 6am.'

With that, Rose and Alex turned to her laptop and started work. John silently packed up his stuff and left the bar. He wished he was the one helping Rose with the investigation. He just wasn't undead enough to be useful.

Chapter 3

John arrived back at Vampires Inc. at 6am as planned. He found Rose brushing her hair in the bathroom.

'Hey John, ready to go to work?' she asked. She looked tired.

'Yep. I guess Alex has jumped back into his coffin now the sun's up, has he?' said John. Rose swung around from the mirror with a cross look on her face. As she did so, John almost jumped backwards in shock. Rose hadn't cast a reflection in the mirror. What was going on?

'Alex was actually a big help last night, so stop being so rude about him,' she said. 'We've got a lead on the Elder who killed Linda. Her name is Philippa Renton and she was turned into a vampire in 1866 at the age of sixty-five by an Elder male. Her patient record was in a locked file that Alex was able to crack into. Dr Jacobs was trying to keep his work on her a secret.'

John followed Rose out to his car. She ignored the pastry he'd bought for her. Vampires never eat or drink, he thought to himself. Rose always wanted breakfast. Something was definitely going on. What had happened to her last night?

****

For six hours, John and Rose sat in silence outside Max Jacobs's house. Rose went out once, wearing black sunglasses, to get John a coffee. She didn't eat or drink anything. More time passed. John almost fell asleep twice. Stake-outs were more boring than he'd ever imagined.

Just as John was about to nod off for a third time, Rose's phone rang. She grabbed it and shook John awake. 'Drive!' she hissed. 'Get to Jacobs's surgery. Alex has tracked down our suspect. She's on her way into Brighton and she's got someone with her.'

As they drove, Rose explained that Alex had asked some friends to carry out a tracking spell on all the Elders in the area. There was only one, hiding out in a cliff-top house ten miles outside the city. Alex's friends had gone to the house. They had seen a girl being held prisoner in a room full of broken mirrors. Soon after, a car with blacked-out windows had pulled out of the garage and headed for Brighton. That was twenty minutes ago. Rose and John had to get to Dr Jacobs first.

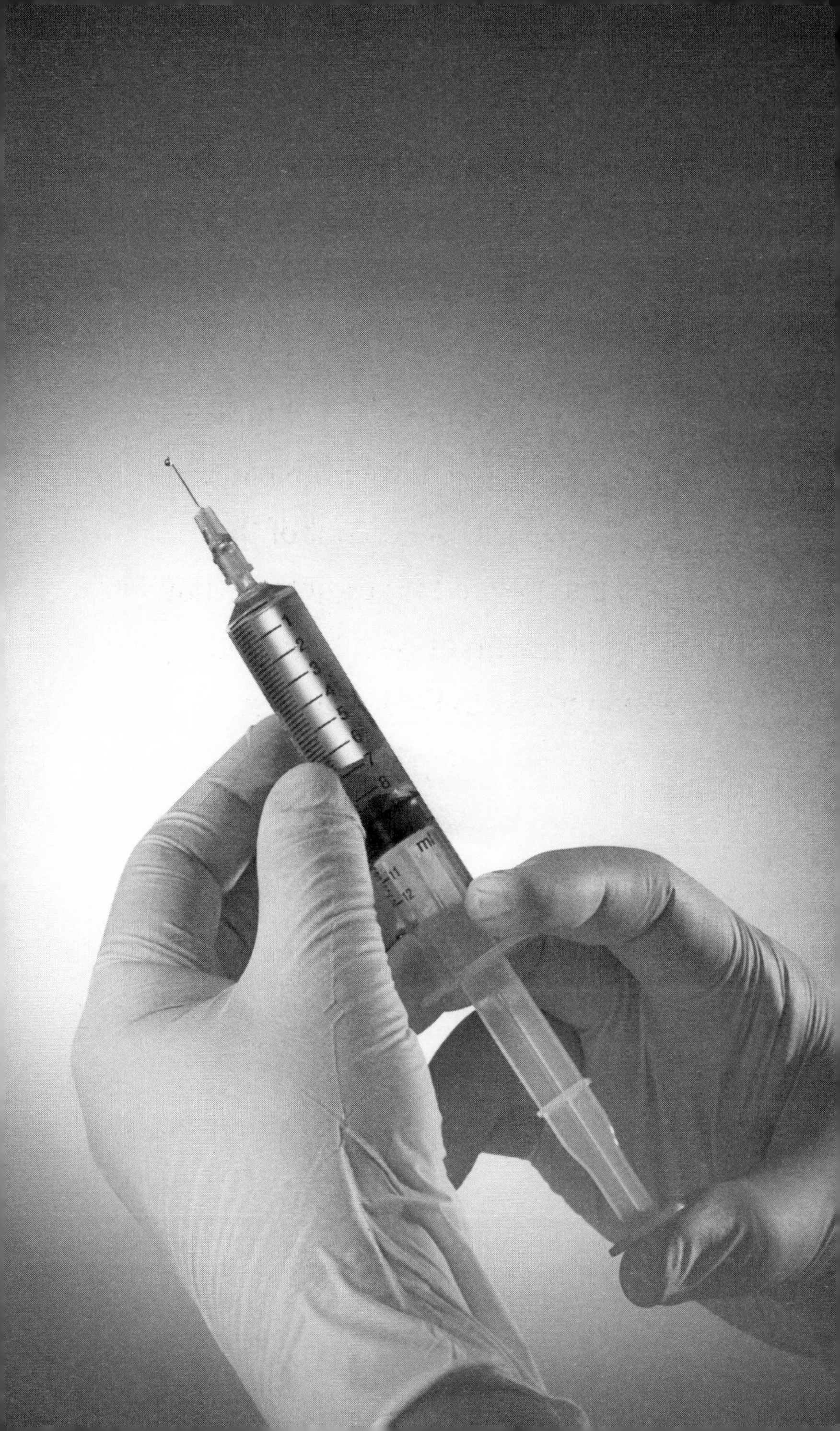
ml

Chapter 4

The wind was howling and heavy rain lashed down on the windows of Max Jacobs's surgery. The doorbell rang. It was his last appointment of the day.

A woman in a hooded cloak stood at the door. Dr Jacobs's new receptionist invited her inside. 'Dr Jacobs will be with you shortly. May I take your cloak or get you a hot drink?'

The woman shook her head. In a rasping voice, she whispered. 'I have brought my daughter with me. She would like to see the doctor as well.'

Opening up the cloak, she pushed Helen Jacobs into the hallway.

A bite mark bled on her neck. Within moments, Philippa Renton had knocked the receptionist out cold. She dragged Helen into Max Jacobs's operating theatre and tied her to the operating table with a rope.

Just then, Dr Jacobs stepped into the room. When he saw his daughter, he gasped, 'Helen! No!' He tried to untie her from the table, but Philippa Renton stood next to her, a wooden stake in her hand.

'One more move, Dr Jacobs, and Helen dies,' she rasped. 'First I want you to look at your handiwork.' Philippa pushed back the hood of her cloak. Her cheekbones and nose were just bones. What was left of her skin was grey and hung in threads from her forehead and chin. Her eyes were hollowed out and black. She really was a monster.

'You must remember me, Dr Jacobs. I'm Philippa Renton. You carried out one of your little experiments with plastic surgery on me. If I'd been turned into a vampire when I was twenty-five instead of sixty-five my immortal life would have been perfect. You told me you could make me young again. Instead, you turned me into a monster!'

'I was wrong!' shouted the doctor. 'I'm so sorry. I thought I could help you. I didn't know the surgery wouldn't work on vampire skin. Please don't hurt my daughter.'

'Oh, I'm not going to hurt your daughter. You are. I wanted you to do this to your wife, but she was so scared of my face she threw herself off the pier. Now get your knives, I want my little vampire girl to look just like me,' laughed Philippa.

Max Jacobs looked down at Helen. Her eyes were dark and her teeth had changed into pointed fangs. She had been turned into a vampire!

'Help me!' he yelled. With that, the windows slammed open and John Logan and Alex Reddy leapt into the room. John held up a metal crucifix and a bottle of holy water.

'Just watch where you're spraying that!' shouted Alex to John, as they backed Philippa Renton into a corner. The vampire cowered from the holy cross that John held close to her. It gave Alex the chance to grab her, but the monster fought back. She slashed at Alex with her blade-like nails.

As Philippa and Alex fought, John saw the wooden stake lying by the operating table. He couldn't reach it but the doctor could. He could use it to destroy Philippa. 'Jacobs! Grab that stake!' he shouted to the doctor. Max had just finished untying Helen from the table. With a superhuman leap, the girl jumped up. She grabbed the stake and threw herself into the fight. Stepping back just in time, Alex gave Helen a clear shot at the Elder vampire.

She thrust the stake into Philippa's chest. There was a scream and a dull bang, then the monster was gone in a cloud of ash.

John held on tightly to the holy water and the crucifix. There was no knowing what Helen might do next. But she just started to shake and cry. Alex wrapped his arms around her and spoke quietly into her ear. Max Jacobs tried to reach out to his daughter, but John gently led him away. Helen had been turned into an Elder – she was part of Alex's family now.

Behind them, Rose staggered into the room. 'What happened?' she said with a groan. She was holding her head. Rose was the 'receptionist' who had been knocked out at the door. When they had arrived at the surgery, Rose, John and Alex had planned to lead Philippa into a trap. Once inside the surgery, Alex would overpower her and take her back to the senior Elders for punishment. Only now, Philippa was gone and he was taking back a new vampire instead.

'It was a shame you missed everything, but John and I made a good team,' said Alex. He looked over at John. 'You can put the weapons down now, mate. It's all over.'

John waved the bottle of holy water near Alex. 'I was so tempted to give you a quick splash of this,' he said with a grin. 'But as you didn't get me killed,

I'll let it go this time.'

Alex smiled and shook John's hand. Then he gave Rose a hug and led Helen out to his van. She waved goodbye sadly to her shocked father. 'Give us some time to help her adjust to her new life,' said Alex to the doctor. 'I'll make sure you see her again.'

Maybe he's not such a bad bloke after all, thought John.

Chapter 5

That evening, John and Rose sat on Rose's sofa and talked about the day. Rose stroked her owl's feathers as she yawned. 'Sorry for being so grumpy this morning, John. I was tired after working all night.'

'That's okay,' said John. He looked into the cup of herbal tea he had made for her. It was empty. 'Rose, did you drink that tea?'

'Of course I did,' she replied.

He looked at her carefully. 'You're sure you drank it?'

'Yes, of course I'm sure. You don't think Alex has turned me into a vampire, do you?' Rose gave John a long stare, then started to laugh. 'Oh, come on! Do you think I'm that dumb?'

John scratched his head. He wanted to say more. 'But what about the bathroom mirror?' he said. 'You didn't have a reflection in it this morning.'

Rose dragged him into the bathroom. 'There was no reflection because there is no glass in the mirror. Danny, my owl, flew into it and broke it last week. If you'd looked carefully you'd have realised that!' she said.

'I'm so sorry,' he said. 'You must think I'm such a fool.'

Rose punched him lightly on the arm. 'Yes, I do think you're a fool. But it's nice to know you care.'

John relaxed and they sat back down in a peaceful silence together. Soon Rose was asleep. Smiling to himself, John realised that he really did care. And he hoped that maybe one day, Rose would care about him too.

Glossary

cowered – huddled over in fear

crucifix – the figure of Jesus nailed to a cross-like shape, usually made out of wood

ignored – when a person takes no notice of you or another thing

immortal – living forever

lab – a place where physical evidence is examined, also known as laboratory

meditating – focusing on your breathing to calm your mind and spirit

plastic surgeon – a doctor who carries out operations to change the way people look

staggered – when a person finds it difficult to walk properly and nearly falls over

Quiz

1 What is the name of the woman killed at the beginning of the story?

2 What evidence does Rose Petal find in the woman's watch?

3 What does the monster do to all the mirrors in her room?

4 Why is the monster so angry with Dr Jacobs?

5 Which vampire helps Rose Petal with this case?

6 Why does John get so frightened when Rose Petal looks in a mirror?

7 What is the name of the vampire who has become a monster?

8 How does the vampire get revenge on Dr Jacobs?

9 Whose family does Helen Jacobs join?

10 What is the reason for Rose's reflection disappearing in the bathroom mirror?

Quiz answers

1 Linda Jacobs

2 Strands of hair

3 She smashes them

4 He promised to make her young and beautiful but it went wrong

5 Alex Reddy

6 He thinks she has lost her reflection and must have become a vampire

7 Philippa Renton

8 By killing his sister and then turning his daughter into a vampire

9 The vampire family of Elders

10 Danny, the owl, flew into the mirror and broke it, so there is no mirror there anymore

About the author

The author of these books teaches in a London school. At the weekend, his research takes him to the beaches and back streets of Brighton in search of werewolves and vampires.

He writes about what he has found.

VAMPIRES
INC.

VAMPIRES
INC.
Hunter's
Moon

VAMPIRES
INC.
Ace of
Spades

VAMPIRES
INC.
Face
Lift

VAMPIRES
INC.
Vampire
Child

VAMPIRES
INC.
Gangs of
Brighton

VAMPIRES
INC.
Vampire
Haters

VAMPIRES
INC.
End
Game

VAMPIRES
INC.
Life is
Forever